DOUG CAN & DOUG WILL

WRITTEN BY CLARE McBRIDE
ILLUSTRATED BY STEFANIE ST. DENIS

Doug Can & Doug Will
Copyright © 2022 by Clare McBride & Stefanie St. Denis

Tellwell Talent
www.tellwell.ca

ISBN
978-0-2288-5153-0 (Hardcover)
978-0-2288-5152-3 (Paperback)

In loving memory of my daughters, Oksana and Quinn, who would have laughed for days after learning the word "dung."

And for my nephew Rory, who shares the same sense of humour with the cousins he never got to meet.

#forever6and4 #dontdrinkanddrive

www.claremcbride.com

"Urgh! Ahhhh! EEEEEEE!"

Doug is pushing hard, but his dung ball just isn't rolling. Doug feels defeated. He can't even do what a dung beetle is supposed to do: roll dung!

"Gggaaaaahhhh!" Doug squeals as he tries once more to push the dung ball along the forest floor with his hind legs. The ball barely moves.

"Argh. I just can't do it," Doug moans as he slumps to the ground against the ball.

It starts to rain.

4

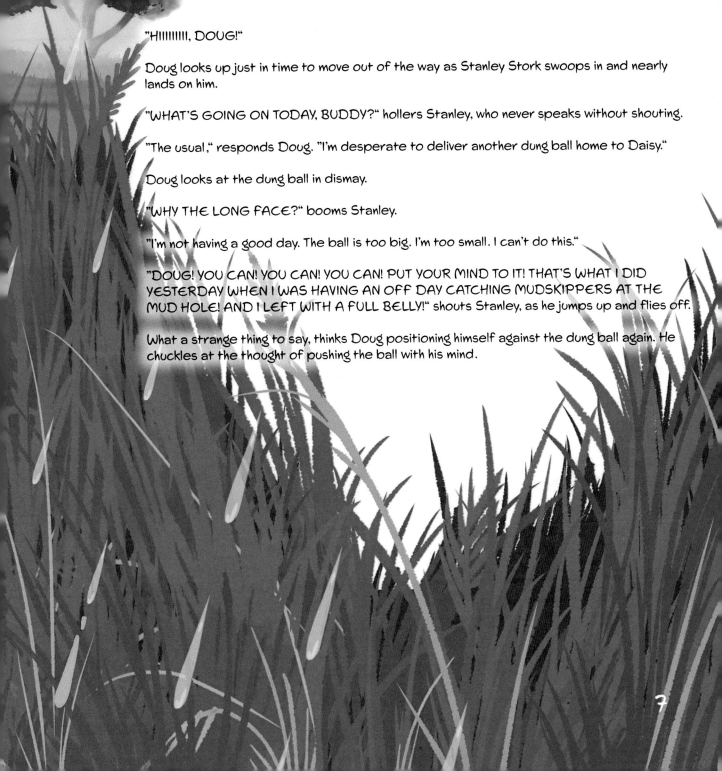

"HIIIIIIIII, DOUG!"

Doug looks up just in time to move out of the way as Stanley Stork swoops in and nearly lands on him.

"WHAT'S GOING ON TODAY, BUDDY?" hollers Stanley, who never speaks without shouting.

"The usual," responds Doug. "I'm desperate to deliver another dung ball home to Daisy."

Doug looks at the dung ball in dismay.

"WHY THE LONG FACE?" booms Stanley.

"I'm not having a good day. The ball is too big. I'm too small. I can't do this."

"DOUG! YOU CAN! YOU CAN! YOU CAN! PUT YOUR MIND TO IT! THAT'S WHAT I DID YESTERDAY WHEN I WAS HAVING AN OFF DAY CATCHING MUDSKIPPERS AT THE MUD HOLE! AND I LEFT WITH A FULL BELLY!" shouts Stanley, as he jumps up and flies off.

What a strange thing to say, thinks Doug positioning himself against the dung ball again. He chuckles at the thought of pushing the ball with his mind.

"Well, if Stanley thinks I can..." Doug mutters.
"ARRRGGHHHH!" he strains.

The dung ball starts to roll.

Pleased that the dung ball is finally moving,
Doug keeps pushing. Suddenly, the dung ball
disappears and up flies a splash of mucky water.

"Oh no!" cries Doug as he realizes that the dung
ball has dropped into a big puddle.

10

RUMBLE! RUMBLE! RUMBLE! Doug knows that sound! He scurries off the path toward a bramble of ferns, so he doesn't get flattened. Edward Elephant's foot lands right in the puddle, sending the dung ball flying all the way back beside the dung pile Doug had rolled it from. Edward doesn't even notice what has happened.

"Hello, Douglas!" says Edward, smiling. "How's it going today?"

"TERRIBLE!" a very frustrated Doug yells, so that Edward can hear him all the way up there.

"What's the matter?" asks Edward, leaning down to listen.

"I'm desperate to deliver a dung ball to Daisy, but nothing is going right today. I give up," Doug moans.

"Doug, you have done this before. You will do it again! Put your mind to it. That's what I did yesterday when I didn't really feel like uprooting any more trees, and I got the job done," advises Edward.

Doug rolls his eyes. Why does everyone keep telling him to push the dung ball with his mind?

11

After walking all the way back to the buffalo dung pile, Doug finds the ball. He backs up to it and PUSHES. The now soaking-wet, misshapen dung ball doesn't move. Doug slouches against it, thinking about his horrible day. It rained, Stanley almost flew into him, and the dung ball fell into a puddle. Then Edward sent the dung ball flying back to where it came from, and they both told him to push the ball with his mind, but Doug doesn't know what that means. Now it's getting late. Doug just wants to see the smile on Daisy's face when he brings home a fresh dung ball!

"I guess I'm just going to have to try again," he mutters. "I've done it before. I will do it again!"

Doug repositions himself. Stanley says he can! Edward says he will!

"I can! I will!" he roars before giving a huge push! The ball budges. Doug is tired but he's desperate to deliver this dung ball, so he keeps PUSHING.

"I can. I will. I can! I will! I CAN! I WILL..."

12

Finally, Doug and the dung ball make it home. Daisy is waiting on the doorstep.

"I was getting worried," she says. She helps Doug push the dung ball into their tunnel so she can start unpacking it to make a new bed!

"Sorry, Daisy. I had a hard day," replies Doug. He tells her how he had such trouble getting the dung ball to roll, and then about Stanley almost landing on him. He tells her about Edward sending the dung ball flying. And then he tells her about their weird advice to use his mind to push the dung ball.

"Interesting," she says, smirking. "So how did you do it in the end?"

"Simple. Stanley said I could and Edward said I would, so I just told my legs that. I repeated 'I can. I will.' over and over agai..." Doug stops mid-sentence. He thinks.

"Ooohhh!" Doug exclaims, suddenly realizing what happened. Repeating his friends' encouraging words in his mind had convinced his legs to keep going!

Doug smiled. He was thankful for encouraging friends and their weird advice. He was thankful he had the strength to 'put his mind to it' and get the job done.

Daisy winked. "Guess your mind did some pushing after all," she grinned.

15

Get to Know Doug!

dung
/dəNG/
noun
the excrement of animals; manure

Lifespan: up to three years
Number of young per hatch: 3-20
Size: 0.5 - 2.5 inches long
Other names: tumblebugs, scarab

Dung beetles, which can be found on every continent except Antarctica, live in farmland, forests, grasslands, the desert, or the prairies. Dung beetles come in a variety of colours from black to green to red. Dung beetles do exactly what you might expect with a name like that! They fly around looking for the dung of herbivores and omnivores such as cattle or elephants. When they find some dung they like, they roll it home where it's used as a food source or to make a bed for laying eggs in. Dung beetles have wings and spurs. They use their spurs for rolling the dung balls home. Some dung beetles can move dung balls up to 50 times their own weight!

18

Manufactured by Amazon.ca
Bolton, ON

29691766R00017